EEK & ACK
BEYOND THE BLACK HOLE

Librarian Reviewer
Katharine Kan
Graphic novel reviewer and Library Consultant, Panama City, FL
MLS in Library and Information Studies, University of Hawaii at
Manoa, HI

Reading Consultant
Elizabeth Stedem
Educator/Consultant, Colorado Springs, CO
MA in Elementary Education, University of Denver, CO

STONE ARCH BOOKS
www.stonearchbooks.com

Graphic Sparks are published by Stone Arch Books
151 Good Counsel Drive, P.O. Box 669
Mankato, Minnesota 56002
www.stonearchbooks.com

Library of Congress Cataloging-in-Publication Data
Hoena, Blake A.
    Beyond the Black Hole / by Blake A. Hoena; illustrated by Steve Harpster.
    p. cm. — (Graphic Sparks. Eek and Ack)
    ISBN 978-1-4342-0759-3 (library binding : alk. paper)
    ISBN 978-1-4342-0855-2 (pbk. : alk. paper)
    1. Graphic novels. [1. Graphic novels. 2. Science fiction.] I. Harpster, Steve, ill.
II. Title.
PZ7.7.H64Bey 2009
[Fic]—dc22   2008006709

Summary: While zipping through space in their rocket-powered washing machine, Eek
and Ack get sucked into a black hole. Moments later, they're spit out on the other side of
space. The new universe has its own planet Earth, but it's a weird pink color. Of course,
that won't stop this terrible twosome from trying to conquer it.

Art Director: Heather Kindseth
Graphic Designer: Brann Garvey

1 2 3 4 5 6 13 12 11 10 09 08

Printed in the United States of America

EEK & ACK

BEYOND THE BLACK HOLE

by Blake A. Hoena

illustrated by Steve Harpster

CAST OF CHARACTERS

EEK

ACK

BLECK

ZEEK

ZACK

5

10

11

Seconds later on the other side of space . . .

FHOOOT

We're still alive!

But where are we?

20

23

31

ABOUT THE AUTHOR

Blake A. Hoena once spent a whole weekend just watching his favorite science-fiction movies. Those movies made him wonder what kind of aliens, with their death rays and hyper-drives, couldn't actually conquer Earth. That's when he created Eek and Ack, who play at conquering Earth like earthling kids play at stopping bad guys. Blake has written more than 20 books for children, and currently lives in Minneapolis, Minnesota.

ABOUT THE ILLUSTRATOR

Steve Harpster has loved to draw funny cartoons, mean monsters, and goofy gadgets since he was able to pick up a pencil. In first grade, he avoided writing assignments by working on the pictures for stories instead. Steve was able to land a job drawing funny pictures for books, and that's really what he's best at. Steve lives in Columbus, Ohio, with his wonderful wife, Karen, and their sheepdog, Doodle.

GLOSSARY

black hole (BLAK HOHL)—an object in space with super-strong gravity. Scientists believe black holes are created when stars collapse.

gravity (GRAV-uh-tee)—the powerful force that draws things toward any large object. Stars, planets, and moons all have gravitational pull.

meteoroid (MEE-tee-ur-oyd)—a small space rock that enters a planet or moon's atmosphere

ooze (OOZ)—what aliens do when they go to the bathroom

universe (YOO-nuh-vurs)—everything that is in outer space

vaporize (VAY-puh-ryz)—to turn something into very small pieces, usually done with a ray gun

whizzler drive (WHIZ-luhr DRIVE)—the engine that propels Eek and Ack's ship through space at super speed

wormhole (WURM-hohl)—a tunnel in space that connects two distant places

Z (ZEE)—the worst grade you can receive on the planet Gloop. It's also the last letter in the alphabet and the name for an alternate universe.

Zearth (ZERTH)—a pinkish version of the planet Earth. Zearth is located in the Z universe.

BLACK HOLE FACTS

A black hole is what's left after a massive star dies. The star's intense gravity causes it to collapse into itself, creating a core. The core has such strong gravity that not even light can escape its pull. It is so dense that it sinks into space-time, creating a hole, which is why we call it a black hole. Black holes cannot be seen.

TYPES OF BLACK HOLES

Schwarzchild (SHWARTZ-sheeld)—a black hole that does not have a rotating core

Kerr (KUR)—a black hole with a rotating core. Kerr black holes are the most common. If a star is rotating when it collapses, then a Kerr black hole is created.

THE SIZE OF BLACK HOLES

Our Sun is bigger than 333,000 Earths. Pretty big, right? Black holes are even bigger! Smaller types of black holes, including **micro black holes**, are about the size of our sun. **Supermassive black holes**, however, can have the mass of billions of stars like our sun. Scientists believe that there is a supermassive black hole at the center of most galaxies, including our own, the Milky Way Galaxy.

WORMHOLES AND TIME TRAVEL

No one knows what happens to an object that is sucked into a black hole. Scientist Robert Kerr had a new idea about some rotating black holes. He believed they wouldn't have the crushing gravitational force of most black holes. Kerr thought it might be possible to enter one of these black ones and then exit through a white hole. A **white hole** would be the opposite of a black hole. Instead of sucking objects in, a white hole would spit them out.

The connection between the black and white holes is called a **wormhole**. Wormholes could connect faraway places in space, or even be doors to alternate universes. However, most scientists think that whatever enters a black hole will be crushed and destroyed.

DISCUSSION QUESTIONS

1. Ack receives a Z on his report about black holes. What's the worst grade you've ever received and why? Do you think Ack deserved the grade he received? Explain why you think so.

2. Eek and Ack are brothers, and they look similar, but in what ways are they different? Use examples from the story to explain your answer.

3. Eek and Ack are space aliens from the planet Gloop. Do you believe there are real space aliens? Why or why not?

WRITING PROMPTS

1. If you flew through a wormhole and ended up in a different universe with another Earth, what would it be like? How would the plants and animals be different from what we have here on our Earth?

2. Eek is constantly thinking up sinister plots to conquer Earth. If you were Eek, how would you conquer our big, blue home? Write it down!

3. Eek and Ack are disgusted by all things pink and fuzzy. Is there something that disgusts you? Describe what you find disgusting about it.

INTERNET SITES

The book may be over, but the adventure is just beginning.

Do you want to read more about the subjects or ideas in this book? Want to play cool games or watch videos about the authors who write these books? Then go to FactHound. At *www.facthound.com*, you'll be able to do all that, and more. The FactHound website can also send you to other safe Internet sites.

Check it out!